cornbread & poppy

for the **win**

matthew cordell

Little, Brown and Company

New York Boston

To Julie, Romy, and Dean—
who won the Winner's Cup of my heart

About This Book

The illustrations for this book were done in pen and ink with watercolor. This book was edited by Mary-Kate Gaudet and designed by Angelie Yap. The series is designed by Joann Hill. The production was supervised by Kimberly Stella, and the production editor was Marisa Finkelstein. The text was set in New Century Schoolbook, and the display type is hand lettered.

Copyright © 2024 by Matthew Cordell • Cover art copyright © 2024 by Matthew Cordell. Cover design by Angelie Yap. • Cover copyright © 2024 by Hachette Book Group, Inc. • Hachette Book Group supports the right to free expression and the value of copyright. The purpose of copyright is to encourage writers and artists to produce the creative works that enrich our culture. • The scanning, uploading, and distribution of this book without permission is a theft of the author's intellectual property. If you would like permission to use material from the book (other than for review purposes), please contact permissions@hbgusa.com. Thank you for your support of the author's rights. • Little, Brown and Company • Hachette Book Group • 1290 Avenue of the Americas, New York, NY 10104 • Visit us at LBYR.com • First Edition: April 2024 • Little, Brown and Company is a division of Hachette Book Group, Inc. • The Little, Brown name and logo are trademarks of Hachette Book Group, Inc. • The publisher is not responsible for websites (or their content) that are not owned by the publisher. • Little, Brown and Company books may be purchased in bulk for business, educational, or promotional use. For information, please contact your local bookseller or the Hachette Book Group Special Markets Department at special .markets@hbgusa.com. • Library of Congress Cataloging-in-Publication Data • Names: Cordell, Matthew, 1975– author, illustrator. • Title: Cornbread & Poppy for the win / Matthew Cordell. • Description: First edition. | New York : Little, Brown and Company, 2024. | Series: Cornbread and Poppy ; 4 | Audience: Ages 6–10. | Summary: Best friends Cornbread and Poppy race in a competitive cycling championship. • Identifiers: LCCN 2023013494 | ISBN 9780316508674 (hardcover) | ISBN 9780316508773 (trade paperback) | ISBN 9780316571890 (ebook) • Subjects: CYAC: Mice—Fiction. | Best friends—Fiction. | Friendship—Fiction. | Bicycles and bicycling—Fiction. | Racing—Fiction. | LCGFT: Animal fiction. • Classification: LCC PZ7.C815343 Cs 2023 | DDC [Fic]—dc23 • LC record available at https://lccn.loc.gov/2023013494 • ISBNs: 978-0-316-50867-4 (hardcover), 978-0-316-50877-3 (pbk.), 978-0-316-57187-6 (ebook), 978-0-316-57188-3 (ebook), 978-0-316-57189-0 (ebook) • PRINTED IN CHINA • APS • Hardcover: 10 9 8 7 6 5 4 3 2 1 • Paperback: 10 9 8 7 6 5 4 3 2 1

◎ Contents ◎

⚙ New Pants ⚙

It was almost time!

The annual Small Rodents Competitive Cycling Championship Classic—the SRCCCC—was tomorrow. Cornbread and Poppy had been training for months.

Cornbread arrived at Poppy's house. He checked his watch.

"Wow! My best time yet!"

The door swung open, and Cornbread could hardly believe his eyes.

"Poppy, your pants!" he yelled.

"You like my new pants?" Poppy was wearing all-new shiny bike gear. New helmet, new shirt, and most noticeably, a new pair of very snug pants.

"Well, yes…," said Cornbread. "Are you sure you got the right size? They look very tight."

"Of course, silly!" said Poppy. "They are supposed to be tight! I got all the best gear because I want to win!"

"I even got a pair for you, Cornbread!"

"Oh…yay?"

Every day at training, Poppy had talked on and on about how much she wanted to win.

She had even been working on a top secret "Master Plan," which she refused to reveal until the day of the race.

Cornbread was enjoying their time together, and he was excited about the race. But that didn't seem to be enough for Poppy.

She had become very competitive.

"Thank you for
the pants, Poppy.
But, you know, it's
okay if we don't win.

TUG!

PULL!

"I'll have fun just
being with you."

"Not win? Not a
chance!" yelled Poppy.

YOINK!

"Besides, we can't let Gerald win again."

Gerald had won the
Winner's Cup at
the SRCCCC for
the past four years.

And he was not
nice about it.

He loved to brag and taunt the other racers about how great and unbeatable he was.

"Ugh, Gerald," said Cornbread.

"Ugh, Gerald," said Poppy.

16

"Gerald is unpleasant at best," said Cornbread. "But no matter what, let's just enjoy the race together, Poppy."

"You said it," said Poppy. "And no matter what, this race is ours!"

Cornbread and Poppy rode out for one last training session.

Sure enough, Poppy did seem a little faster.

"Maybe she's right about this new bike gear," thought Cornbread.

"See, Cornbread! Tight pants for the win!"

⚙ The SRCCCC ⚙

Early the next morning, before the sun had even come up, Cornbread was brushing his teeth when he heard a knock at the door.

"Good morning, Poppy," said Cornbread.

"The time has come to reveal the Master Plan!" Poppy said, charging through the door.

"Here's what we need to do. We start out fast
but not too fast. And we keep that same
fast-but-not-too-fast pace for most of the race.
All the way till the final lap. Then we give
it everything! We really have to punch it,
Cornbread!"

22

Poppy had a tiny, wrinkled piece of paper
scribbled with notes and drawings.

"Um…okay, Poppy. Sounds…good?" said Cornbread. "Would you like some breakfast? I've got our favorite oatmeal on the stove."

"No time!" said Poppy. "We've got to get to the race and set up!"

"We cannot race without breakfast!" Cornbread insisted.

So Cornbread
finished getting
ready…

…then he and Poppy shoveled
down their oatmeal.

26

Off they rode, to the starting line of the race.

"Not too fast!" shouted Poppy. "We don't want to waste all our energy before the SRCCCC!"

And there it was....

The WINNER'S cup!

It was glorious, big and golden, and decorated with jewels and sparkles, and it was being polished up by none other than Pound Cake himself.

"Hi, Pound Cake!" said Cornbread and Poppy.

Pound Cake was Moonville's all-time greatest, nicest racer.

He held the record for most wins at the SRCCCC, and eventually he retired so other rodents could have a chance to win.

Everyone loved Pound Cake.

Everyone, it seemed, except for…

…Gerald.

"I'm coming after your record, Pound Cake," said Gerald.

"Just a few more wins and I'll have more Winner's Cups than anyone. See you at the finish line, slowpokes!"

"Ugh, Gerald," said Cornbread.

"Ugh, Gerald," said Poppy.

"Ugh, Gerald," said Pound Cake.

This year's race seemed larger than ever.

Lots of small rodents were lining up. There were mice, squirrels, chipmunks, rats, muskrats, hamsters, gerbils, and guinea pigs.

With all the cyclists here for the race,
Cornbread wasn't feeling so confident.

Poppy, however, still fully expected to win.

It was finally time for the racers to begin.

"Don't forget the Master Plan, Cornbread," whispered Poppy. "Strategy for the win!"

"Okay, everybody!" shouted Old Larry, the town grump and official starter of the race.

"This better be good!

On your marks…

…get set…

And the race was on!

Each and every small rodent quickly charged ahead of Cornbread and Poppy. But this was all according to Poppy's plan.

In the first lap, a chipmunk
firmly held the lead.
But she used up too
much energy too soon.
She promptly pooped
out and fell behind.

A muskrat and a gerbil blew
their tires and fell out.

Cornbread and Poppy inched closer to the
front of the race, still pacing themselves.

In the second lap, a hamster took the lead. He was overly confident, though, and ran himself into a mudhole.

CRASH!

A rat, a guinea pig, and a squirrel had a multi-bike pile-up on the next turn.

Cornbread and Poppy stuck to the Master Plan. And they moved even closer to the front of the race.

On the third and final lap, out of the cluster of cyclists, Gerald emerged.

Like Cornbread and Poppy, he had been saving his energy until the end. And, oh no, he was coming up fast!

"We can't let Gerald have it!" yelled Poppy.
"Punch it, Cornbread!"

They exploded past the other racers,
but Gerald was now neck and neck with
Cornbread and Poppy.

The finish line and the Winner's Cup were all
within reach around the last turn.

And then…

Cornbread's special pants ripped wide open.
His too-tight pants suddenly had been pushed
to their limit, and they split apart, flapped
about in the wind, and were promptly sucked
into the spokes of his wheel.

flop
flip
flap

"NOOOOO

Cornbread flipped head over heels and smashed himself and his bike into Gerald. Then a gerbil, a chipmunk, a squirrel, and countless other racers collided with them. It was a pile-up!

It happened so fast that Poppy could barely
make sense of it all. She had somehow cleared
the entire crash, and she was still going at top
speed. She was so, so close to the finish line.
Poppy would win the race if she kept going.

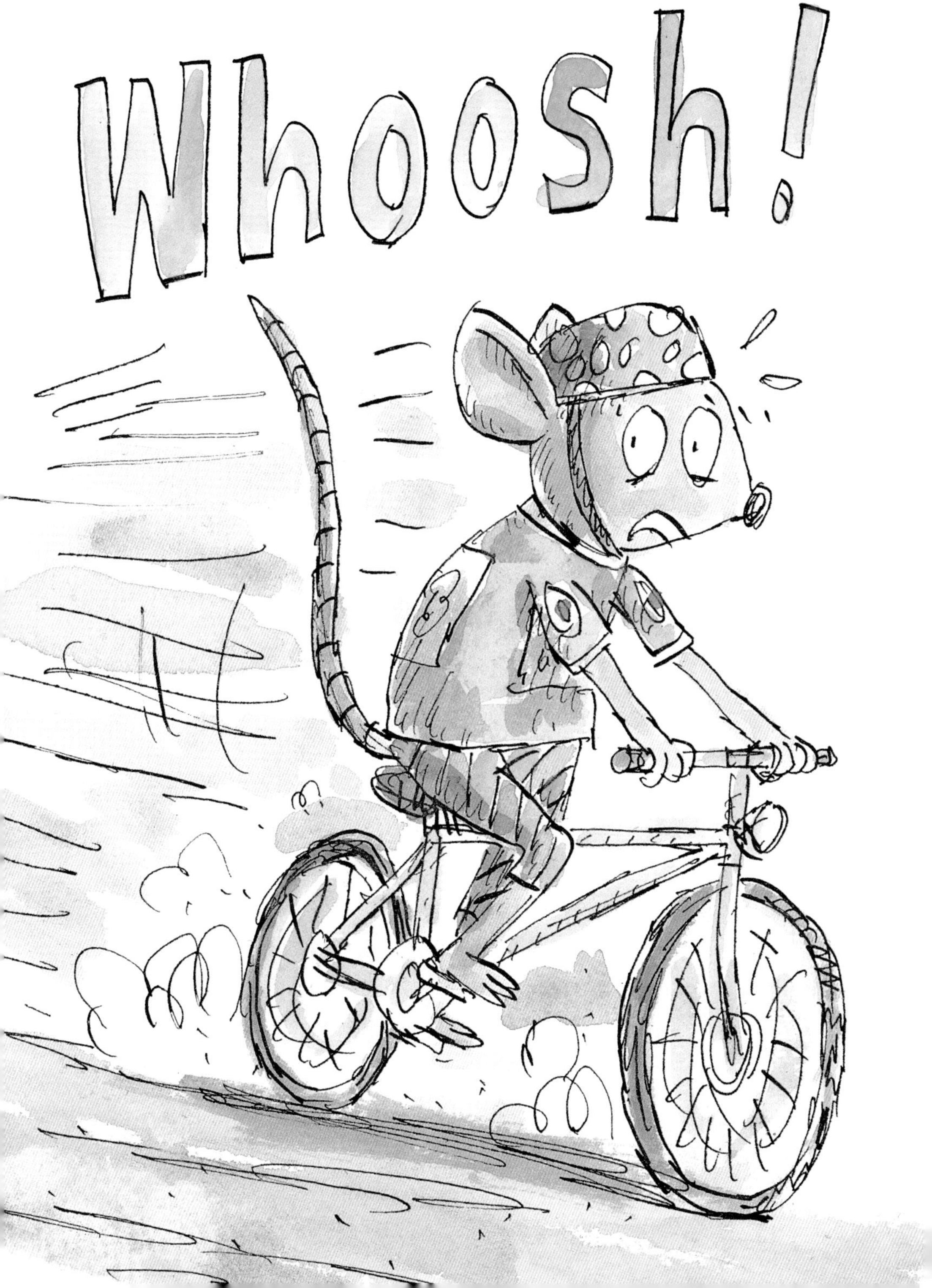
Whoosh!

But Cornbread was lying flat on his back. He wasn't okay. They all looked pretty bad. And it all made Poppy feel bad.

She even felt bad for…ugh, Gerald.

S-K-K-K-K-K-K!!!

Poppy hit the brakes. She skidded to a stop.

She couldn't leave her friend like this.

As all the racers gathered themselves and their cycles, the slowest, smallest racer, Moley LaRue, made her way past the pile-up and over the finish line to claim the Winner's Cup.

SQUEAK - SQUEAK - SQUEAK....

⚙For the Win⚙

With a borrowed pair of Pound Cake's pants,
Cornbread hobbled back onto his bike.
Poppy followed in silence.

It was an awkward ride home that evening.
Between Cornbread's bruises and Poppy's
bruised ego, they didn't know exactly what
to say.

The next morning, Cornbread heard a tap at his door. He was too tired and sore and sad to answer.

"Hello," said Poppy. "I let myself in. I wanted to check on you, and I brought our favorite oatmeal to share."

"Ouch...hello, Poppy. Thank you."

"I…I'm sorry, Cornbread."

"You're sorry? I lost the race for us, Poppy.
I feel horrible. You should be celebrating with
the Winner's Cup right now. Why did you
come back for me?"

"You were right, Cornbread. The SRCCCC got the best of me. And I didn't see it until I left you there in the dust. Having fun together matters more. Friends matter more. You matter more than any silly, shiny Winner's Cup."

Cornbread sat up.

"Ouch…Thank you, Poppy. You are a good friend."

"And you are a good friend," said Poppy. "Friends for the win!"

"Yay!" said Cornbread.

"Oatmeal for the win!"

"Yay!" said Cornbread.

"And NEW new pants for the win!" said Poppy. "Gotcha these for when you're feeling better."

RUSTLE
RUSTLE